# Jilted Widow

# Jilted Widow

Iridescent Toad Publishing

Iridescent Toad Publishing.



Cover design by Valdas Miskinis.

First edition. ISBN 978-1-913779-35-1

*The things to be seen*
*By the light of the moon*
*The gentle*
*The eerie*
*And the downright sinister*

# Chapter One

Under the scorching hot sun, the bumpy road had made for a laborious and uncomfortable journey. Fray sighed. It had been far too long since he'd had a drink and he was gasping for one. Desperate to get some kind of relief from the clammy discomfort of the day, frustrated, he wound the window right down. He was grateful to feel a rush of air as it came in at him, hitting his glistening bare chest. The sounds coming from the woods reminded him that he was very far off the beaten track. It was late in the day and he could hear crickets chirping; their unmistakable din seemed far more prominent than any birdsong ever could. It was so humid out in the country that it was probably too hot for most birds.

The headache-inducing pressure in the air signalled to Fray that a storm was probably due. The thought didn't provide him with the relief he needed though. The road ahead looked never-ending and just as cumbersome as the current one. A lack of traffic was such that there were no streetlights to lead the way. It wasn't a problem for now, but it would be when sunset occurred; he would have to drive more carefully then. With just his headlights to rely on, it would be a tentative journey indeed.

*What was that noise?*

A strong gust of wind charged along the edge of the trees that overlooked the road. The motion was so sharp that through the leaves that shifted, a residential building became suddenly visible through the gaps. The chimney was tall, its crookedness evident against the backdrop of the sky.

Fray proceeded to drive at an even slower speed but it wasn't long before he could see a stony road. It certainly wasn't the widest of roads but nevertheless it was one that he could drive on if he wanted to. He figured that if he followed this stony road into the woods, it could take him to the house that he had just seen behind the trees.

*Surely if the weather takes a turn for the worst, someone might be willing to take in a lodger for the night,* he thought to himself.

Deciding to take his chances, Fray turned the steering wheel in the direction of the woods. Just as he started to fear that his wheels would give way to the multi-textured ground underneath, the large house became suddenly apparent in his field of vision.

Fray pulled up next to the house. It was situated behind a gate of iron bars, far too tall for even a stealthy person to be able to climb over. At the very peak of them, next to an expertly crafted stone gargoyle were two letters, *F.F.* Behind the iron bars was an abundance of overgrown shrubbery. The grounds looked very uncared for. *Maybe the house is an abandoned one?* Fray wondered.

As he twisted the key out of the port near the steering wheel, Fray cringed. He was anxious that whether or not his old car would start again was always going to be a lottery. He willed himself to stay calm and focused.

Catching sight of himself in the wing mirror, he noticed how exhausted he looked. The bags under his eyes were dark and deep-set, despite the fact that he was reasonably handsome overall.

Remembering that he had a clean shirt in the back of the car, he went to put it on straight away. He figured that if he was going to ask a stranger for help then he at least needed to look presentable.

As another breeze billowed past him, Fray was grateful for how cooling it felt. Equally though, it brought home to him how late it was getting. The trees danced in multiple directions as the fickle change in weather revealed the moon. It was a full one – bright and bold.

Hoping that his car would be ok in the makeshift parking spot, Fray walked cautiously towards the gate. As he pushed it open, it sounded just as rusty as it felt. It was heavy and unforgiving.

As he walked towards the house, it was only then that he appreciated the full size of it; it was so looming and overbearing that it was more like a mansion than a house.

The walls were coated in plant life that was clearly out of control. The unforgiving ivy contrasted with the peeling paintwork. It was dry and brittle, just like the balcony and the pillars that dominated the exterior structure. Distinctively, the windows were all closed and the door looked firmly locked. Fray grew all the more concerned that the house had been abandoned.

The moon was so bright that even though it was getting dark, Fray still had just enough light by which to look around. He noticed that despite how the garden was in disarray, the lavender bushes were still in full bloom. As he looked at the soft hues of purple and blue, it turned his thoughts to how much he missed his girlfriend. He had often picked wildflowers as a gift for her and had always treated her well. Nevertheless, she had left him. He should have seen it coming; she wanted money but he had been out of work for some time. The thought made him reach out to touch one of the lavender stems.

Suddenly, a frantically loud banging noise diverted his attention to the top of the house.

Looking around cautiously, Fray noticed a woman at the far end of the garden. She was willowy and thin. Her frail silhouette was enhanced by a veil draped over her head that flowed all the way down to her feet. The veil moved with her in the wind whilst the brightness of the moonlight made her features difficult to distinguish.

The woman seemed to be on high alert, as if she was looking for something – or someone – in particular. Fray was keen to ease the tension. Just as he started to walk towards her, he stopped dead in his tracks. The woman moved with such a domineeringly vicious energy that upon sensing it, Fray quickly darted behind a large bush.

The woman glided towards him, as if on an invisible tramline. Her slight stature was such that as soon as she turned towards the house, she was swiftly out of sight.

*Maybe whoever owns this place might be grateful for some help around here. It sure looks like it is in need of some care*, Fray thought to himself. *If I could just find whoever lives here, maybe I could speak to them about it. There could be a job in it for me.*

As he walked onto the porch, Fray was very aware of how much the wooden steps creaked under his weight. They didn't feel sturdy, or even stable. The house was so tall that all of the windows were large. He took the opportunity to look through one of them. Although it was coated in grime, he was able to lean forward enough to see inside. The only light was that which came from a single candle that had been placed further into the room.

Bracing himself as he noticed the gargoyle on the brass knocker, he banged it against the door assertively.

Nothing. No response.

He tried again.

Still no response.

Curiosity getting the better of him, Fray nudged the door to find that although it was heavy, it wasn't locked.

As soon as he took his first step into the building, he was taken by surprise by the sound of a cat hissing. Although it was black and almost camouflaged against the darkness of the room, the glint in its marble green eyes drew attention to its entire silhouette. Its back was arched angrily and the ash black fur that adorned it stood on end. The animal was ready to strike and Fray would have been foolish not to notice.

More amused than afraid, Fray stepped forward.

"I'll be damned if I'm going to let something as small as an angry cat scare me away," he whispered to himself.

Notably though, his heart was beating faster now that he was inside the house. He was scared to let the door close behind him. Something about doing so would have made him feel trapped.

Although the eerie feel of the house was vivid, Fray willed himself to proceed forwards.

"Is there anybody home?" he shouted out into the darkness.

The silence that greeted him was almost more noticeable than it had been before.

Everything in the house looked so dated. There was no phone and no television to be seen. All of the furniture – ranging from tatty to broken – was from a time gone by. It looked as if it had been kept in the house for a very long time indeed.

Further ahead, Fray noticed that there was another room to be explored. The door was open to reveal a painting that was visible by a chink of moonlight that must have been coming in from a nearby window. The subject of the painting was a woman dressed in rags. Her posture looked just as worn as her clothing and yet despite whatever her predicament was, her expression displayed a smile that was almost menacing.

Fray was impressed with himself; he had managed to make out the details on the painting despite how the glass covering it had an almighty crack right in the centre. It looked as if someone had administered a vicious blow to it with something sharp and pointed.

Distracted by all of the unusual details about the piece, as Fray moved closer to inspect it, he read aloud the name that was burnished onto the brass at the bottom of the frame.

"Black Widow."

The name made him curious. As someone who was interested in nature and always happy to be outdoors, he had read about the black widow. The female spider with a venomous bite. Predatory, self-serving creatures willing to trap their prey and devour them slowly and painfully once it was time to feed.

It unnerved Fray to wonder who on earth would want such a painting in their home. It was of a large and overbearing size. The woman's crooked smile – foreboding and unavoidable – dominated the room. Nothing he had seen so far had unnerved him in quite the same way, and certainly not to the same extent.

Feeling that he had come too far to turn back, Fray continued to look around. Instinctively, he set his sights on the candle in the next room. As it sat flickering alone, Fray identified it as a source of guiding light.

As he realised that the fireplace was on, it concerned him tremendously. It had been such a hot day that it didn't make sense for anyone to have it on and yet, the absurdity of it added to his curiosity. Not too far from the fireplace was an abandoned table. Someone had clearly used it recently. The fruit bowl was overflowing with fresh grapes and red apples. Furthermore, there was some kind of pâté that appeared to have been enjoyed not too long ago; it certainly didn't look or smell like it had gone off.

A single set of cutlery looked as if it had been slammed down on the table with urgency whilst someone was part-way through their meal. Fray felt guilty to think that perhaps he had disturbed someone who might have just wanted to be left alone. *Maybe she was expecting someone round for dinner*, Fray mused as he noticed that the table had been set for two, even though it had clearly only been used by one.

He chuckled to himself at the absurd thought that maybe whoever it was had been expecting him.

Seeing the bottle of wine on the table reminded Fray of how he still hadn't managed to quench his thirst. Normally he wouldn't be so forward, but the opportunity of a drink was too good to resist. Drinking straight from the bottle, he raised his brows, impressed at how good the wine tasted. It slipped down his throat and provided him with some relief, as much as he would have preferred it to be water.

With the house being so poorly lit, it was clear to Fray that he needed to make a decision. *It must be getting late,* he thought. *This is uncomfortable. Maybe I should leave. I could turn back and sleep in my car.*

"What were you doing in my garden?" said a soft female voice.

Fray had been so deep in thought that he hadn't noticed the woman enter the room.

Although her voice was quiet and she was stood behind him, Fray could sense her presence now. He quickly turned around. He was pleasantly surprised at how pretty she was. She was pale with long dark hair. Her long flowing dress added to her mystique. Not only that, but her face was difficult to make out due to the fact that it was partially adorned with a translucent veil. Her voice was so sweet. Fray couldn't understand why she would want to hide away.

"I'm sorry," said Fray. "I admit that I am trespassing. I promise I mean you no harm though."

"You should think about how your intrusion could make other people feel," said the woman indignantly, but not angrily.

"I didn't mean to upset you," said Fray. "I've been on the road for so long and when I noticed the path to your home, I wondered if it could be a place for me to stay. I didn't know what to expect and I took my chances."

"Oh? Really?"

The woman's voice sounded so peculiar to Fray. Despite the fact that her presence commanded the room in a way that was almost overwhelming, the way she spoke sounded broken and would be barely audible to anyone refusing to listen carefully enough.

Before Fray could continue with his train of thought, the unmistakeable rumble of thunder broke outside.

"I'm Fray," he said.

He extended his hand towards the woman in the hope that he could break some of the tension.

The woman paused uncertainly before recoiling away from Fray. She did so deliberately enough to make it clear that she didn't want to shake hands with him.

"It's clear that you need a room for the night," she said.

With that, she lit a candle and carrying it with her, she walked ahead leaving Fray to follow her. As he watched her move so gracefully, it astounded him to think that she seemed so alone in such a large place. They passed many rooms as they moved down the large hallway.

"Sleep here for the night," said the woman, motioning towards the door at the end of the hallway.

"I'd like to repay you for your hospitality," said Fray. "I notice that the house, and indeed the garden, needs quite a lot of work doing to it. Is there anything I can do to help? I promise I'll be careful and that I'm experienced enough to do a good job."

Fray was so used to being out of work that trying to persuade someone why they should accept his services came naturally to him.

"I'm not sure," said the woman, a sadness in her eyes. "I'll give it some thought."

With that, she turned away and glided softly back down the hallway, the darkness becoming more apparent to Fray as she took the candle with her.

Taking the opportunity to get his bearings of the bedroom as best as the moonlight would allow, Fray looked out of the window. The storm was still at full aggression with the rain pelting down. It bounced off the leaves on the trees and a spray of condensation was visible on the ground.

Feeling too exhausted to weigh up whether or not he was fully comfortable with the situation, Fray sat on the bed and it wasn't too long before he was settled down and fast asleep.

# Chapter Two

The sun's rays streamed in through the window. It was early in the day and already it was clear that it was going to be a hot one.

As Fray stretched out on the unfamiliar bed, through tired bleary eyes he drowsily began to look around. Although he had managed to sleep right through the night, his dreams had been awful. In his mind's eye, he had seen the same thing over and over again; images of the woman running around the manor in a hysterical state. Maniacal. Agonised. She had looked horrendously distressed, screaming with the most tortuous blood-curdling angst.

With the generously bright sky having vanquished the dark stormy blanket of the night, Fray was able to look out of the window properly for the first time. The sheer height of it went in his favour. He could see for what seemed like miles.

Beyond the garden, there was a lake. With a dark green tint coating most of its surface, it looked deep and undisturbed, possibly even stagnant. It disappointed Fray to think that taking a dip in the coolness of the water would be a bad idea. Just between the garden and the lake was what looked like some kind of memorial. There seemed to be a headstone in the middle and it was surrounded by lots of smaller stones. There were no flowers though. Nothing that made it look cared for, respected, or even recognised. Fray made a mental note to himself that there were probably just some places that were meant to be left alone.

Even though the storm had passed and the grass still had a light dew on it, the garden seemed to be shrouded in an atmosphere of discomfort and distress. Fray thought back to the horrible dreams he'd had – the screams and how frantically pained the woman had sounded.

He had no idea what the day ahead had in store for him but telling himself that it was a new opportunity, Fray walked across to the bathroom. He figured that it would be good to shave while he had the chance.

Running the palm of his hand across the emerging beard on his chin, once in the bathroom, Fray was stunned to notice that the mirror was cracked. The shape, size and position of the cracks were similar to the damage he had seen on the painting of the ragged woman. Suddenly feeling very uncomfortable about the whole thing, he decided that just one more day of stubble wouldn't be a problem at all. Not wanting to think about the mirror, he drew a bath.

There was a part of him that didn't want to spend any longer in the bathroom than he absolutely had to but the water filled the tub quickly enough and although it didn't reach the ideal temperature, Fray was grateful for it nevertheless. He laid back and enjoyed the cooling relief of the water against his skin. He didn't care that the bath hadn't been used in a while to the extent that it made the water a little grimy. He had put up with worse.

Once back in the bedroom with a towel wrapped around him that he had found near the bathroom sink, Fray was surprised to see that there was a dressing gown on the bed. *That's strange*, he thought to himself. *There's no way that it could have been there before.* He felt very on edge but did his best to reason with himself that the woman must have heard him in the bathroom and taken it upon herself to put the robe on the bed –

ready for him – during that time.

The dressing gown was a lovely deep plum colour. Full length with plush long sleeves. It felt soft and comforting against Fray's skin. It had been a while since he'd experienced something comforting. He was grateful for it.

He looked out of the window again, curious to become more acquainted with his surroundings. He noticed that the black cat seemed to be toying with something. Upon closer inspection, it was a mouse. Just a couple of metres away, stood the woman. She was watching the cat with a fixed smile on her face, almost as if she was proud of its will to mutilate the poor mouse.

Fray took the opportunity to remind himself that his stay at the house only needed to be a temporary one.

The dressing gown was so comfortable that Fray kept it on as he went downstairs. He was confused to observe that the table had been set for breakfast. An array of delicious-looking fruit adorned elaborate bone china plates. It certainly looked excessive for a mere breakfast, even if he was a guest.

The woman was nowhere to be seen. Fray took it as a hint that she didn't want to spend any time with him. He found it odd that she would go to the trouble of catering for him when she was so keen to avoid him but nevertheless, he was hungry and so decided to tuck in.

As he pulled out a chair from the table and went to sit down, he froze on the spot, horrified to his very core. The glass over the Black Widow painting was now in perfect condition. It was unlike how it had been when he'd first set eyes on it.

*But how... how is that possible?* he wondered. *The house is in the middle of nowhere and who could have got in and fixed the glass so swiftly and so quietly – and all without being noticed?!*

"You seem very taken by that painting."

Hearing the woman's voice behind him, Fray shuddered. He looked up to see her stood in the doorway, her willowy silhouette commanding the whole room.

"I have given some thought to your offer," she said. "You may do some work on the house. I'll pay you when you're finished."

It annoyed Fray that the woman was so aloof with the details but without anything else lined up, he figured that he may as well take his chances.

"I see you've had the glass on the painting repaired," said Fray, hoping to find out what had happened.

"Apparently so," said the woman.

She was frustratingly vague. Fray didn't dare to ask her any more questions. He didn't trust her to tell him anything with openness and candour anyway. *Maybe that's just her way,* he told himself.

He couldn't have asked her more questions even if he had felt confident to. Whilst his eyes had been on the painting, she had already left the room.

# Chapter Three

Fray spent the next few days working hard on the house. The resources that his host provided for the job were limited, but just about enough. Sometimes when he hammered the nails too hard into the wood, it would splinter and split to the point that his efforts felt futile. Other times he would manage to make, albeit slight, enough of an improvement to things that he felt he wasn't wasting his – or his host's – time.

He felt looked-after even though the woman's hosting style was more than a little strange. She always served him good food but never sat down to eat with him. Sometimes the food was waiting on the table for him and other times she would serve it to him and leave the room, swift and cat-like as if trying to avoid being caught for some unknown reason.

There were moments when the woman seemed to value Fray's company though. Although she

was a closed book and often said very little –
even if asked a direct question – she had got into
the habit of asking Fray to walk with her in the
evenings. Through the garden they would go, in
a silent companionship that wasn't quite
comfortable but wasn't completely awkward
either.

One evening, as much as Fray found it difficult
to understand, he didn't complain when the
woman reached out to hold his hand. Upon hers
making contact with his, he was shocked at how
cold her skin felt to the touch. *How can someone
feel so cold even on a warm summer's eve?* he
wondered.

His uncertainty didn't go unnoticed by the
woman. So much so that when he flinched, it
greatly offended her.

The two of them walked back to the house in a
state of frigid silence. Nothing more was said
that night.

# Chapter Four

Over the next few days, Fray and the woman didn't communicate at all. Not a word was spoken and not the slightest amount of eye contact was made. Nevertheless, every day began with Fray coming downstairs to find that the woman had made breakfast for him. She always made sure to leave fresh fruit and a pot of hot tea on the table. Her timing was excellent; she managed to have everything ready for Fray but in such an efficient manner that she was out of the house by the time he was downstairs.

On some of the mornings, Fray looked out of the bedroom window and saw the woman wandering around the garden. She seemed to float aimlessly like a lost soul. There was a melancholy about the way she moved even though she was not the most expressive. Her arms were always down by her side and her pace – whether she was moving fast or slow – never seemed to falter or be uneven. Fray could never tell whether the woman knew that she was being watched. If she did, she did an excellent job of not letting on. She seemed far away and in her own world.

Fray couldn't understand why the woman seemed to roam the garden without purpose. She didn't seem to be looking for anything and she never tended to the lavender or the weeds. Her wandering seemed aimless and yet for her, so necessary. Fray had almost become so used to it that even though there was something about it that seemed unnatural, he had come to expect it.

He shook his head, keen to snap out of his reverie. He endeavoured to remind himself that no matter how strange the goings on at the house seemed and no matter how weird the woman's behaviour was, upon completing the work that had been asked of him, he would be out of there and hopefully better off than he had been before. He still had no idea how much the woman would pay him but on the basis that he had nowhere else to go, he had no choice but to hope that he wouldn't be leaving the house empty-handed. Besides, all of the jobs that the woman had given him so far hadn't been unreasonable. Hammering and painting had all been part of what was necessary.

He still hadn't quite become acquainted or indeed comfortable with being in the company of the black cat. It would often appear behind him when he least expected it. *When it comes to stealth, that cat is in a league of its own,* Fray thought to himself. He wasn't even sure if the cat was male or female because he simply hadn't been able to get close enough to it. He didn't really want to either.

34

# Chapter Five

Having resigned himself to the fact that he needed to get on with the job, Fray awoke to good weather. Perfect for going up on the roof to fix the tiles.

Although he knew that the climb up to the roof would be rickety and tentative, he had done his best to secure the structures on the porch the previous day. As a result, he reasoned that if he could climb up onto the roof via the side of the house that was near the porch, it would be his best bet for getting up that high safely. The height of the house was such that it would not lend itself to a safe fall down. He couldn't take any chances.

Sighing and reminding himself that he would run a nice hot bath after the long day's work, Fray made sure to gather everything he would need. He wanted to be sure that he wouldn't have to go up or down the ladder any more times than absolutely necessary, especially seeing that there was nobody around who he trusted to hold it. He felt that he just couldn't ask the woman. There was something about her, when she was walking the garden, that unnerved him to the point that the last thing he wanted to do on such occasions was get her attention. There was something about her manner during her walks that made him fear that he could enrage her. He didn't want to see what she might be like if angered, not after the recurring nightmares that he'd been having about her.

*I won't have to be here for much longer,* he told himself.

Fray's dreams about the woman had been particularly distressing over the last few nights. In them, he had seen vivid visions of her looking more and more distressed, her screams piercing his mind and the contortions of her face appearing terrifying and yet unavoidable. In the dreams, Fray desperately wanted to look away. But he couldn't.

The vividity of the dreams was such that sometimes, Fray would find himself waking up convinced that the woman had just been whispering in his ear. And yet every time he darted out from under the duvet, there was never anybody there.

As Fray carefully stepped up on each rung of the ladder towards the roof, he promised himself that he would work quickly. He didn't want to be at the house for any longer than necessary and in particular, he was keen to get the roof over and done with in one day.

If it wasn't for the fact that there was a leak in the roof, Fray might have considered skipping that part of the job entirely. He didn't want to insult the woman's hospitality or intelligence though – the damp on the inside walls directly under the worn parts of the roof were an absolute giveaway. It would only take one more storm for streams of fresh rainwater to taint the wallpaper once more.

Once at the top of the ladder, Fray breathed a sigh of relief. He could see what needed doing and faced with the most problematic part of the roof up-close, the task at hand didn't look as daunting as he had feared it could be. Mentally marking out the parts that needed his attention the most, he placed everything he would need in the open guttering that ran horizontally alongside the roof.

*I should be able to get this done before sunset,* he decided optimistically.

# Chapter Six

Cautiously blinking his eyes open, Fray didn't know where he was. All he could see in front of him was pale blue sky. It did nothing to help his disorientation. He had no idea why he was flat on his back and no idea what had happened. It must have been something painful though. His whole body ached and the pain in his back and his neck was such that he was scared to move, fearing that it could cause him more pain.

He was startled to realise that, for the very first time since he'd arrived at the house, the black cat was sat right beside him. The soft fur brushed against his bare arm. The cat even nuzzled his head into the crook of Fray's elbow.

*Why has the cat warmed to me all of a sudden?* Fray wondered.

Slowly and carefully turning his head to try and make sense of things, Fray realised that he was on the grass. Behind the cat, he could see the house. It dawned on him that he may have had a fall. He wasn't sure though.

Turning his head back to face upwards due to the pain he could feel from moving his neck, Fray was so startled that a yelp of shock escaped from his very core.

Stood over him was the woman. Her face was expressionless.

"You fell off the roof," she told him in a matter-of-fact tone.

"When? How?" he asked.

"We'd better get you inside."

With that, she passed a walking stick down to him and before he could ask her any more questions, she was once again out of sight.

Frustrated, he sighed. *Surely she could have been a bit more helpful – just on this one occasion!*

Fray knew that he was on his own and wouldn't be given any help to get up, no matter how much he needed it. There was nobody else around for miles. He knew that shouting would be futile.

Carefully rolling over onto his front, he scooted onto his knees and then got up as gradually as he could. He still felt dizzy. Even though he was annoyed at how aloof the woman could be, even in a situation like this, she was right. Fray knew that with the pain he was in, staying outside wouldn't do him any good at all.

Storm clouds began to gather. Fray took this as a sign that he must have been unconscious on the ground for quite a while. As he turned to walk into the house, the cat followed him, more concerned about him than the woman had been.

"Animals are always more sensitive than most people can be," Fray muttered to himself.

# Chapter Seven

A good night's sleep did Fray a lot of good. So much so that he managed to remember what had happened to him just before he'd found himself on the ground and staring up at the sky in a daze.

His dream about what had happened had been so vivid that he was convinced that it was a clear explanation of events…

Whilst at the top of the ladder and working on the roof, he had heard a sudden loud banging noise. It had startled him and made him jump. The way in which his weight had shifted on the ladder was such that it had slipped from underneath him and had taken him tumbling down with it. Fray knew he was right. In his dream recalling the event, he had felt his gut catch in his chest as gravity betrayed him prior to the long fall. As his now-bruised back had hit the ground, it had knocked the wind right out of him. And then, nothing. Total darkness until he had noticed the black cat brushing up against his arm.

As he lay there in bed and the sun's rays punctuated the room, Fray's head was full of questions. *Why was there such a loud banging noise? Why did the woman seem so knowledgeable about what had happened to me? Why didn't she help me up? I haven't done anything to upset her. Does she want to hurt me? This doesn't make sense!*

Fray figured that he had a number of options but he couldn't quite get his head around which combination of them would cause him the least trouble. By asking the woman outright what her game was, it could result in him being sent away with no payment for the work he had done so far. By continuing to work on the house in the current conditions – without voicing his concerns to the woman – then surely he was keeping himself in some sort of danger.

Fray didn't like his options. He felt annoyed at himself. He had always had the propensity to prioritise being a gentleman over asserting himself. As a result, it had cost him dearly in the past and he was anxious that the same thing would cause him problems with the woman.

*It's never simple is it?* Fray thought to himself as he threw his hands up in exasperation and then drummed them down on the old duvet that cocooned his aching body.

Even throwing his hands up had caused a jolt of pain to surge through Fray's back. The pain reminded him that in his current state, he didn't feel fit to drive away. He certainly didn't feel that he was in a fit enough state to run if the woman turned out to be even more difficult than she had shown herself to be already. With that in mind, as much as he felt uncomfortable and as much as there was a part of him that feared for his safety, Fray figured that his best bet would be to stay compliant. At least, until he was well enough to make a dash for it if things were to turn impossibly sour upon him telling the woman that he would be leaving.

*And what of the housework? I can't do that in this state!* Fray worried.

Fortunately, he didn't have to fret about that for much longer.

The woman drifted into the room so casually that Fray didn't notice her presence until she was stood at the foot of his bed.

"You poor man," she said, the empathy in her voice not quite convincing. "You should rest here for a while until you're better."

"But what about the housework?"

"That can wait," she said.

And with that, she was once again out of the room.

It confused Fray to think that the woman didn't seem at all concerned that he would be out of action for a while. She didn't seem to be in a rush to get him to leave and yet, she didn't seem that bothered as to whether the work on the house got done or not.

Fray didn't know what she was up to, but he was more convinced than ever that it wasn't good.

# Chapter Eight

S leep comes often to the wounded and Fray was no different. Having dozed off not long after the woman had left the room, he awoke to find that a bowl of fruit had been placed on the chest at the foot of the bed. He made the assumption that the woman must have left it there for him.

"Why put it all the way over there?" he complained to himself in a quiet frustration.

No matter how much he wanted to overlook the woman's strange ways of trying to get his attention, Fray couldn't stop thinking about her. He couldn't stop dreaming about her either. Once again his sleep had been punctuated by sounds and images of her smashing reflectionless mirrors in a state of pained hysteria. In the dreams, sometimes the woman's face had been terrifying to see and yet Fray was unable to look away. Her horrific expression would sometimes melt into an anger that made her look relentlessly ghoulish; almost like a cursed soul who would stop at nothing to harm those who had wronged her.

Fray thought back to how the woman had seemed to delight in watching the black cat toy with a mouse. He had seen the softer side of the cat but as far as he could tell with the woman, there was something perhaps bitter – and maybe even sadistic and twisted – about her. *Why else would anyone delight in watching a cat taunt a mouse?* he asked himself.

The bowl of fruit at the end of the bed was too tempting to deny and as much as Fray didn't feel up to trying to reach for it unassisted, there was no way that he was going to shout for the woman. He was at the point where, as far as he was concerned, the less he saw of her, the better.

Tentatively, Fray attempted to move. At first he tried to reach across to the end of the bed with just his arm outstretched. He figured that this way, it would be the least uncomfortable for him. He was wrong. He felt a sharp shooting pain in his lower back. Infuriated, he realised that he would just have to get out of bed entirely and take his time in doing so. After sighing heavily and psyching himself up to move, he carefully twisted around into a sitting position until the soles of his feet were touching the floor.

Taking care to stand up gradually, Fray was relieved to notice that although he still ached all over, he was able to slowly walk towards the chest at the end of the bed. He felt glad that he had needed to push himself to get out of bed; it served as an opportunity to assess whether or not he was in a fit enough state to be able to escape the house at short notice should it be necessary. There was still a part of him that very much wanted to. Unfortunately though, it was evident that running would be agonising and that it wouldn't be possible to get very far.

*What use would it be to run away if it would only anger the woman? – especially if the odds of her catching up with me are pretty high!*

As he enjoyed the crisp, fresh sensation of biting into a juicy red apple, Fray was startled to notice that the woman was stood watching him in the doorway. Her face was expressionless and yet she seemed to be transfixed on his every move.

Fray was too angry to hold back his words.

"What on earth is wrong with you?! Why do you

creep up on me like that?!"

The woman didn't answer. She simply turned around and went away.

Fray couldn't tell if he had enraged her or if she had been calm about his outburst. She hadn't given much away. Despite his hunger and despite how good the bite of the apple had tasted, he angrily threw the fruit down at the floor with such force that it shattered into small pieces.

Too livid to eat or drink, he plonked himself down on the edge of the bed and swore at how the swiftness of his movement had caused him more pain. Putting his head in his hands, he sighed. He couldn't make head nor tail of what was going on.

*Why is the woman so kind and helpful in some instances and yet so unbearably impossible in others?* he mused.

# Chapter Nine

Still shaken up as he sat on the edge of the bed, Fray was hoping that the woman would leave him alone. He was worried that he might have upset her but there was nothing he could do about it. He couldn't go back and undo his outburst and so he would just have to accept the consequences of it, whatever they may be.

He had just about managed to calm down when suddenly, he heard an almighty noise.

It was exactly the same noise that he had been hearing in his dreams. Glass shattering. The sounds of an impact delivered with rage.

He couldn't hear any screams from the woman though. It confused him because based on how vivid his dreams had been, he was almost expecting to hear her.

Without giving it a second thought, Fray stood

up and – despite the pain he was in – walked slowly to the bedroom doorway in the hope of being able to see or hear what was going on.

Once again he heard what sounded like the aggressive smashing of glass. Despite his reservations, instinctively he proceeded to walk down the hallway. He wanted to find out what was going on.

Regret immediately washed over him as he got to the doorway of the room where the woman was. She was stood in the centre of it, surrounded by glass but with not a cut or a trace of blood on her. She certainly looked dishevelled though. Before Fray could process what was going on, the woman charged towards him, screaming maniacally with an expression on her face to match.

Instinctively, Fray swiftly extended his hand to strike the woman. In the heat of the moment, he had no other option. She stopped just before she was within an arm's length of him though. Her face looked almost distorted with anger but her eyes burned right through into Fray's very core.

Fray wanted to run, but he couldn't. Even if his injuries would allow, he was too frightened to turn his back on the woman. The danger of the situation was overwhelming and he didn't know if he would be capable of reasoning with her.

"This is just like the dreams I've been having," he rambled, dazed and confused. "I don't understand. What?! Why?!"

The woman laughed at him menacingly. She seemed satisfied that she had finally got a reaction out of him. Her smile was a bitter and twisted one.

To the side of her was a wooden chair. Suddenly, she grabbed it. With a force of strength greater than her slight appearance implied, she held the whole thing up over her head. She looked as if she was about to launch it at full force in Fray's direction.

"STOP!" he shouted at the top of his voice.

He was rarely one to shout but there was nothing else he could do.

The woman didn't hesitate to put the chair down. As she backed away from Fray, she looked almost relieved that someone had dared to confront her.

Sensing that he wasn't completely safe but refusing to back down, Fray walked towards the woman. He wanted to show her that he wasn't afraid. He also wanted to show her that there was nothing for her to be afraid of. He figured that something must have been seriously upsetting her for her to have got into such a state. He felt sorry for her. Although she still looked menacing, Fray sensed that something must have made her snap somewhere along the line and it must have been incredibly unpleasant.

The woman backed further away from him until she was stood in the corner of the room. She still looked angry enough that if pushed emotionally, she could charge at Fray in the most vindictive of ways. Equally though, he felt that he had no choice but to try and calm the situation.

"Do you do this often?" he asked.

He immediately smirked with embarrassment at how stupid his question must have sounded to the woman. He didn't want to insult her. It was clearly a delicate situation.

The woman glared at him, a volatility in her eyes that reminded him that he couldn't afford to say the wrong thing.

"Would you like me to help clear the mess?" he asked.

The woman's expression softened. Whilst she didn't seem to care about the damage she had done, she looked grateful that someone cared enough to offer to clean up.

Fray had become used to female hysteria. His ex-girlfriend had had her moments and his mother and sisters had never been the most stable of personalities. His familiarity with dealing with some of the most bizarre of situations had always been something that he'd anticipated would serve him well. He was still afraid of the woman in front of him but there was a part of him that wanted to help her, even if it was motivated by his own interests. He wanted to get paid and to get away from the house safely.

"You break a lot of glass, don't you?" he said, trying to find out more but not wanting to seem like he was prying.

The woman didn't say anything.

Fray knew he needed to take the lead. He refused to let himself be manipulated.

"Wait there," he said. "I know where the dustpan and brush are. I'll go and get them and I'll be straight back."

Still the woman said nothing. Fray was certain that if he couldn't help her, he at least wouldn't want to leave her in a worse state than when he had arrived.

# Chapter Ten

As Fray rummaged around for the dustpan and brush, something dawned on him; *The only thing that needs clearing up is the shattered glass on the floor. She hasn't broken anything else in the room. It's as if she only wants to destroy the mirrors and the glass on the portraits. But why?*

# Chapter Eleven

Fray took his time walking back to the room. With the dustpan and brush clamped tightly together in his right hand, he was very aware of how they could be utilised as a weapon if necessary. He desperately didn't want to think that things would get to that point but equally, he felt that they could. It made him shudder to think of how the woman had glared at him as she had stood taunted by her own hysteria and surrounded by the shattered glass.

The cat was nowhere to be seen. Fray wished that the creature was there. To have even an animal bear witness to the situation was something that Fray would have welcomed, if only to be able to assure himself that he wasn't going mad. *What kind of person would do such gratuitous damage to their own home?*

He entered the room carefully and, as much as he didn't want to admit it to himself, ready to attack. With his heart thundering against his chest, he couldn't quite believe it. The woman was no longer there.

*Surely not? She must be in here somewhere!*

Fray took great care to check every possible place that the woman could be hiding. He was surprised at how anxious he felt; he even looked in a cabinet cupboard for her!

"This is ridiculous!" he growled.

It annoyed him that he had succumbed to such an extent of paranoia, all on account of what was quite possibly the woman's self-indulgent attention-seeking.

*But surely there has to be more to it than that? It can't just be attention-seeking? Not if she's hysterical. Not if she is so truly disturbed by whatever it is that's bothering her?*

Fray was certain that he had scoured the room thoroughly. There was nothing more that he could do to find the woman. Looking for her would mean going on a long and uncertain errand around the estate. In Fray's poor state of mobility, it didn't make sense to him to take the risk, especially considering the look in the woman's eyes when she had glared right at him.

He limped over to the table where he had enjoyed a good number of breakfasts at the house before things had taken an uncomfortable turn for the worst with the woman. Just as he pulled out a chair to take a rest and get his thoughts together, he spotted a note on the table. There was no pen or ink to be seen nearby. It unnerved him to think that it had just unexplainably appeared. It certainly looked very pointed towards him though. Tainted with age, the paper curled upwards. It was impossible to ignore.

Fray brought the paper up to his nose, curious to know if it harboured a scent as aged as it looked. It was just as musty as the house overall, if not more so. He was convinced that merely touching the paper tainted his fingers with years' worth of dust.

There was a part of him that didn't want to read it, but he knew that he had to.

*It's never easy to explain anything in life and the content of what is hereby enclosed is no exception. I apologise for any discomfort that this may cause you but nevertheless, something brought you here to me and I simply can't ignore what the fates may have wanted to do in my favour.*

*You remind me of my former husband in every way. You're much kinder than he was though. You don't ignore me and you don't tell me about all the ways in which I fail to compare to her, his other lover. The cruelty of his treatment of me has haunted me for many years. I can't so much as catch the smallest sight of my reflection without wanting to break the glass. I'm sorry. I really can't help it.*

*Unlike my husband, Fred Fanara, I don't want to hurt you Fray. I want to keep you here. Even your name would perfectly match his initials on the gate that surrounds the house. Please say you'll stay.*

*I didn't want to become attached to you like this. I tried so hard to ignore you. But you're here. And I feel that what fate has dealt me must be embraced.*

*Please tell me that you'll never leave. I don't want to have to kill you like I killed him.*

Slamming the piece of paper down onto the table, Fray felt the blood drain from his face and down towards his toes. He felt sick but now he knew that regardless of his injuries, he had to escape.

# Chapter Twelve

Fray had only made it as far as the garden before he found himself limping in agony. He desperately wanted to get back to his car at speed and then drive away promptly. The money wasn't important to him anymore. Neither were the niceties of looking for the woman to say goodbye. He had always been wary of her but never in his wildest dreams had it crossed his mind that she could be a murderer.

He didn't dare to think about how on earth she might have killed her husband but it made Fray feel sick to know that he had spent so much time with a woman who was clearly calculating and probably narcissistic too. All things considered, she certainly seemed controlling. For every person betrayed by a lover, it wasn't normal to seek revenge of such magnitude.

Fray wanted to keep running but he had to stop for a moment in order to alleviate the pain in his back. No amount of fear could help him push through it. Instinctively on high alert, he turned around to check that the woman wasn't following him.

And there she stood – at the other end of the garden!

She had her back towards him. Fray knew that if she managed to clock him, it would only take a matter of moments for her to catch up with him. He needed to hide. And fast.

Fray also knew that if he continued to run in the direction that he was headed in, he would continue to be in the open and the woman would spot him. It was time for a detour.

He thought back to the basic geography of what surrounded the house and remembered what he had seen when looking out of the bedroom window. *The bushes leading towards the lake! They are my best bet!* Fray concluded frantically.

He wasn't sure if once by the lake there would be anywhere for him to go thereafter. It was very possible that it would lead to a dead end. Fray was reluctant but knowing that he would certainly be seen by the woman otherwise, he moved as quickly as he could to avoid her potential line of sight.

Stumbling across the uneven ground, Fray eventually found himself at the lakeside. He was too afraid and on edge to sit down but he stretched as best as he could to ease his muscles, conscious that moving too elaborately could blow his cover. The lake was surrounded by bushes and tall trees. He knew that if the woman was actively looking for him then he wouldn't have much time to make a move. If she was calculating enough to manipulate him in the way that she had done so already, Fray trusted that she would leave no stone unturned in her search for him.

Fray took some deep breaths and reminded himself that the more familiar he was with the space around him, the better his chances of escape would be. He promised himself that as horrible as things felt, he would stay where he was until nightfall if it meant that he would have the cover he needed in which to be able to run back to his car.

"The stone memorial!" Fray gasped, forgetting how much he needed to remain unnoticed. "Could it be...?"

*Surely this can't be where her husband is buried? What murderer would be so twisted as to bury someone so lovingly thereafter?!*

The contrast was hard for Fray to understand, but then the woman and her motives overall had been impossible for him to understand too. The more he thought about it, the more it made sense to him that maybe, just maybe, the stone memorial near the lake had been erected by the woman for her husband.

Bracing himself for the worst, Fray bent forward to read what was on the headstone. It was covered in ivy and mud dust. In some ways it looked unkempt but nevertheless, the lakeside seemed to be a peaceful choice of burial location.

Although the engraving on the stone wasn't as sharp as it probably had been initially, it was clear enough that Fray was able to read it without any trouble.

*Fred Fanara*

*1845-1876*

*R.I.P.*

*How can that be?* Fray mused, exasperated. *Whoever made this headstone must have made one hell of an error when engraving it. Surely it should say 1945 to 1976?!... Hang on though... That would mean that the woman looks too young to have been Fred's wife all those years ago!*

Fray jolted upright, backing away from the headstone as if being close to it would cause him harm.

The way the woman had moved... The way she'd avoided him... The way she couldn't physically help him when he'd had his fall... The way she had an innate ability to startle him by coming and going without any natural continuity... The way she always seemed like she was gliding rather than walking and the way that her facial expressions were always more rigid than flexibly animated... And her eyes... Her deep-set staring eyes...

Fray was afraid to admit it to himself but there was only one possibility. It dawned on him in a way that made the colour drain from his face and the very tips of his fingers and toes tingle in dire discomfort.

He'd been staying in the house with a ghost.

# Chapter Thirteen

Fray knew that he couldn't stay by the lake. As he had feared, it was nothing but a dead end. Even if he was in a fit enough state to swim, the condition of the water was just as appalling up-close as it had appeared to be from afar. Not only that, but Fray had no way of being able to tell where the lake would lead to – a gated area or a route through which he could escape. He had no choice but to turn back away from the lake and the memorial. He would have to go back through the garden.

He desperately didn't want to go through the garden. He knew that the odds of the woman catching sight of him were far too high. He was frightened that she would be angry with him, or maybe still hysterical, or maybe in such a state that she would do something to compromise his chances of escape, or perhaps even survival!

Fray anticipated that the woman *would* see him. He told himself that even if the pain of running through his injuries was unbearable, he would need to keep going in order to escape. *The pain won't matter as long as I get out of here,* he promised himself.

Turning to look through the gaps in the bushes, Fray decided that it was time to skirt around the edge of the garden rather than going across and over it. He began to wonder just how intuitive the woman could be. *Does she have the power to see things in a way that I can't?*

Fray knew that he didn't have time on his side and that even though he couldn't afford to get this wrong, he couldn't stop to think about it too much either. Certain that the coast was still clear, he began to edge his way out of the bushes until he could feel the soft carpet of unkempt grass beneath the worn soles of his boots.

It was a windy day. It moved the fog in a way that made it harder for Fray to know what could be up ahead. It scared him to think that as a ghost, the woman would surely have some sort of advantage over him in the circumstances.

*Focus Fray, focus!* he told himself.

As he continued to skirt around the edge of the

garden, he was confident that he was heading in the right direction. Taking a look at the house, with everything he now knew, it looked sadder than ever. Abandoned. The sight of a sorry story that nobody had cared to investigate. *The land could be put to good use if someone cared enough to demolish this awful place once and for all,* he pondered.

Fray was reminded of the poor state of the garden when he felt a stick snap noisily underneath him.

"Shit!" he said aloud, not really thinking about it.

Ironically, it was *his* hysteria that caught the attention of the woman.

Fray heard her before he saw her. An almighty guttural scream filled the air. It was just as deep as it was shrill and certainly otherworldly. It terrified Fray to think that what he had encountered before must have just been the tip of the iceberg in terms of what the woman was capable of.

Turning his head frantically, trying to locate where the sound was coming from, he could see that the woman was charging towards him.

Although she was at the other end of the garden, her intentions were unmistakeable. Her hands were raised high above her head and her entire posture made her look more looming and domineering than ever before. The expression on her face was full of a septic hatred.

Fray turned to run.

"Shit! Shit! Shit!" he panted, frustrated that he couldn't run any faster.

His feet pounded against the ground, each movement causing him a new pain in his hips and lower back.

"It's not important. Push through it," he chanted to himself through the gasps of breath that steamed up in front of him in the cold air.

As he kept running, he could see the gate in his line of sight. *Nearly there, nearly there,* he promised himself.

He desperately wanted to look behind him but he knew that he couldn't afford to. He had no idea how fast the woman could move and he didn't want to find out the hard way.

As the iron bars of the gate loomed closer, Fray could see the initials above it. *F.F.... Fred Fanara!*

"Her husband!" he exclaimed.

It terrified Fray to think that there was absolutely no way he could have imagined any of this. It was all too cohesive and in line with what the woman had put in her letter.

Fray could see his car and soon the gates would be behind him. And that's when it hit him;

"My keys! My keys!" he shouted desperately. "I haven't got my car keys!"

He had no choice but to keep running. Past his car and all the way down the very road he had followed to take him to the house, the evil woman, and her despicable ways.

*Yes, evil,* Fray thought to himself as he pounded down the long road. *There is no other word for it. No matter what hurt her when she was alive, there must surely be some cursed hold over her that keeps her so bitter in death.*

Fray kept running. Through his panic, in his

thoughts he could see flashes of everything he had encountered in the house.

*How apt that of all the paintings that could have been in her house, there was one of a woman by the name of Black Widow.* Fray shuddered to think of how bitter and twisted the woman must have been to identify with something like that. In life and in death.

As he got to the end of the road and past the trees, Fray was met with the main road. It was still a lonely one, but nevertheless it felt like it belonged to a different world compared to where he had just been.

Without his car and with just the clothes on his back, Fray had no idea what he would do next. There was no way that he was going to risk turning back though, not a chance! It amused him to think that some might think him mad to abandon his car in such a way. But he knew better. He felt frustrated, of course. But overall he felt safe knowing that he would never allow himself to set foot beyond the large iron gates of the house ever again.

****